# December is for Christmas

Story *by* ANN SCOTT

Pictures *by* ALCY KENDRICK

WONDER BOOKS • NEW YORK

Jeremy was like other rabbits except for one thing. He could read. It happened one cold December day when he was walking through the forest and saw a piece of paper on the ground. It was a page from a first-grade reader. Jeremy went over and looked at it. And he found that he could read!

The young rabbit quickly ran home to his burrow. "Come here, everybody!" he called. "Mama, Papa, Uncle Alva, Uncle Mike, Uncle Stanley, Grandma, Grandpop, Aunt Agnes, Aunt Beatrice, Aunt Matilda — come here!"

When all the family had come, Jeremy spread open the paper. "Listen," he said. "I can read."

And he read from the page of the first-grade reader:
*"Look, Dick,"* Jane said. *"Look up. Do you see it? I see it."*

When he had finished, Uncle Alva shrugged. "Who's Dick? Who's Jane? See what?" he asked.

"And what for?" Uncle Mike added. "What do they want to look up for?"

"If that's reading," Uncle Stanley said, "I don't see the good of it."

"Nor I," Aunt Beatrice agreed. "It doesn't change a thing — not a thing."

And all the rabbits went back to doing just what they had been doing before Jeremy could read.

Still, Jeremy couldn't quite believe that reading wasn't good. Maybe if one found the right piece of paper, it *would* change things.

So Jeremy went to the edge of town. And he *did* find a piece of paper. He picked it up and rushed back home. "Come here, everybody!" he called. "Mama, Papa, Uncle Alva, Uncle Mike, Uncle Stanley, Grandma, Grandpop, Aunt Agnes, Aunt Beatrice, Aunt Matilda — come here!"

When all the rabbits had come, Jeremy began to read: *One bag of red berries, tree, one package of icicles, one box of snow, one silver star.* That was all there was on the paper.

Uncle Alva wiggled his ears back and forth. "One box of snow!" he snorted. "Who wants to put snow in a box?"

"A package of nonsense, if you ask me," Uncle Mike agreed.

Aunt Beatrice shook her head. "It still doesn't change a thing — not a thing."

The next day Jeremy went to town again. This time he looked outside the school. He found a piece of paper with writing on it and he read it. He read it all the way through. Then he rushed back home. "Come here, everybody," he called, "come here, come here!"

When the rabbits had come, Jeremy began to read. He read slowly, watching his family out of a corner of his eye: *Sarah Jones. Grade Two. What is Christmas? Christmas is a holiday that comes in December. People give presents and sing songs in the snow. They decorate a Christmas tree. First, they find the nicest fir tree they can find. Then they put trimmings on it, and icicles and snow and other things that are beautiful. Last of all, they put a star at the top of the tree. Then they kiss each other and say, "Merry Christmas! Merry Christmas!"*

When Jeremy had finished, all the rabbits sighed happily.

Uncle Alva grinned. "That changes things some, doesn't it?" he said.

"Yep," Uncle Mike agreed. "That's more like it."

So then and there all the rabbits went out into the forest. They called together the other animals, and just as Sarah Jones had said they should, they looked through the forest for the nicest fir tree they could find.

It was on the top of a hill, the tree they wanted, standing alone, pointing into the sky.

"Finest tree I ever saw," Uncle Alva said. Then he turned to the other animals. "Well, what are you standing there for? A Christmas tree has to be decorated, doesn't it?"

So the animals ran and brought back red berries and scattered them over the tree. They hung icicles down from the branches. They gathered great pawfuls of snow and sprinkled it until the whole tree glistened.

Uncle Alva chuckled. "Remember about the red berries and boxes of snow that Jeremy read? I think that that was all about Christmas, too!"

At last, all the animals stood back and looked at the tree.

"It's pretty, all right," said Uncle Mike admiringly, "but it seems as if there's something missing. Read what Sarah Jones says again, Jeremy."

So Jeremy did.

When he had finished, all the animals were quiet.

Uncle Alva sighed. "There's no star," he said finally.

And where would the animals find a star? Where would anyone find a star? It was evening now, and getting quite dark.

So the animals just sat and looked at their beautiful tree and felt sad. Without a star, it wasn't truly a Christmas tree — not the way Sarah Jones had said.

But there was one thing the animals didn't know. Wonderful things can happen at Christmas time. And behind the tree, on the other side of the hill, something was beginning to happen now. The evening star was rising in the sky.

"Just can't take my eyes off that bare spot on the tree," Uncle Alva said.

The evening star climbed farther and farther up the sky in back of the tree — higher and higher. Then all at once it burst into sight at the tip of the tree. And it clung there — right on top of the bare spot.

The animals gazed at the star in wonderment.

"Now I understand that first piece Jeremy read," Uncle Alva whispered softly. "Remember? *'Look. Look up. Do you see it? I see it.'*"

Then all the animals kissed each other, just as Sarah Jones had told about it. They kissed Jeremy twice . . . because, after all, it was his reading that had changed things.

"Merry Christmas!" they said. "Merry Christmas!"